WATCHING YOU

LANCE ERLICK

Finlee Augare Books (Chicago)

This is a work of fiction. All of the characters, organizations, and events portrayed herein are either products of the author's imagination or are used fictitiously, and any similarities to actual persons, organizations, or events is entirely coincidental. Also, though locations used in this work exist, for dramatic effect details have been altered. Accordingly, they should be considered fictitious.

Finlee Augare Books, Chicago, IL
ISBN: 978-0-9889968-8-5 (print)
ISBN: 978-0-9889968-6-1 (e-book)

Printed in the United States of America

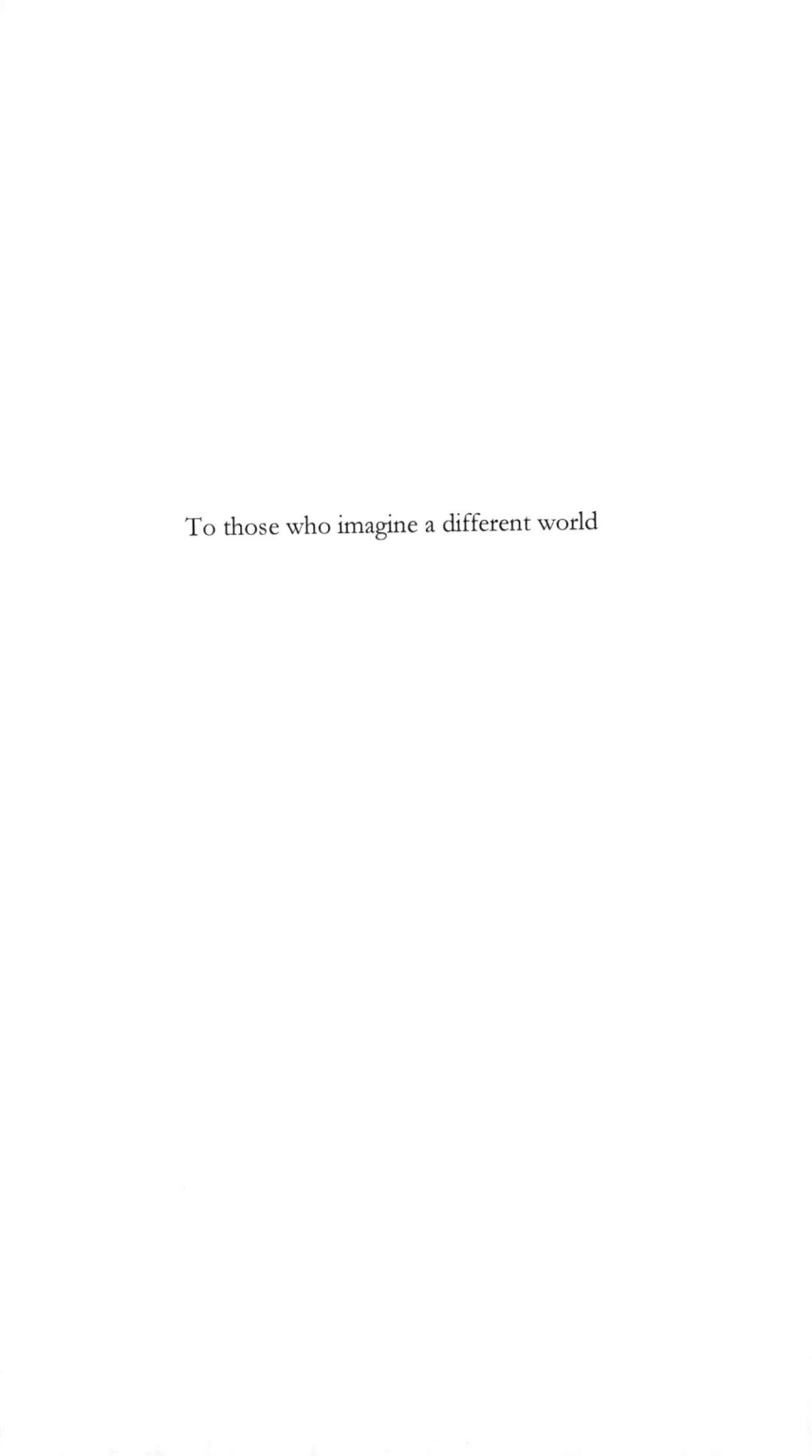

To those who imagine a different world

Harold Winters is fearful when he gets up in the morning and when he goes to bed at night, on his way to work and coming home, and certainly at work. He fears threats he sees on his home vid and those the Standards Board pays him to watch at work. Like other citizens, he puts his trust in Phase V of the Patriot Act, inaugurated after yet another failed terrorist attack.

Sitting in his Patriot Blue cube, third row, fourth down, at the Federal Civil Standards Board, Chicago Office, Harold keeps his eyes on his 42-inch screen lest he miss another imminent threat. Onscreen are nine live views displayed by Art-Intel, the controller supplied by Livermore International Network Corporation (LINC). *Omnipresent INC*, Harold says only to himself. He strains to remember a time before LINC replaced the Internet/web so it could record and sift trillions of vid and voice feeds from all across America.

As a Patriot Blue, Harold is a bona fide second-class citizen with no choice of jobs. He settles for what is offered: playing second fiddle to an artificial intelligence. The last time he saw his parents, they begged him not to resist as they had. Instead, he should adapt to a society that requires all citizens to have RFID implants. When his parents fled, the Standards Board reclassified them to Underclass Red and then Outcast Gray.

Harold couldn't attend their funerals because Outcast Grays and Patriot Blues can't mingle. Of course, Blues know they can't aspire to Privileged Green or, LINC forbid, Honorable Purple, except for Cora Thompson. She is the sweet honey-haired woman on his screen acting in a Board-approved morality sitcom. Though she was born Patriot Blue, the Board upgraded her to Privileged Green so she could act.

Harold's chair vibrates. "Back to work!" The artificial voice carries the unmistakable bass of his boss, Mel Gardner. Someone chuckles nearby. Harold cannot see who it is over the partitions.

Convinced that Art-Intel could do his job, he glances up to look for cams, but of course, they are microscopic. He scans the row of blue plastic plants he suspects serve to hide cams he hasn't yet found.

Returning his attention to the screen, Harold zooms in on one of his nine views. *Have to remain vigilant for terrorist threats.* He is amazed at how Art-Intel culls through so much data, linking searches, purchases, and personal connections to tag someone as a threat. He likes to trace backward to figure out how the clues fit, and what Art-Intel saw that he didn't. Mel ridicules him for being inferior to a biochip.

Onscreen, a dark-haired Patriot Blue woman hardly seems a threat. She sends a cute redheaded girl into the scan-chamber entry for Kerr-Mart, a universal store accessible to Patriot Blues. The girl enters the store. Thick Plexiglas doors lock, trapping the woman inside the chamber.

"Access denied!"

Splitting screens, Harold pulls up her file. There it is— she had an abortion. How could she be so wicked to deny her sweet child life? Harold shakes his head. *That must be a mistake.* The child is there, frightened, staring at her mom.

"Your status is downgraded to Underclass Red," an artificial voice tells the woman.

A brown-shirt escorts her daughter away. Harold pulls the child's file. A Privileged Green couple wants to adopt this redhead, but the mother refuses to give up her only child. This will open doors for the child like when they upgraded Cora. *Good for you.*

The dark-haired woman pounds on the Plexiglas barrier keeping her from her retreating child. Harold wishes he could tell her the good news. When the redhead tries to run to her mom, the brown-clothed guard picks her up and carries her down a long corridor to a waiting van. The woman's anguish tugs at Harold. Not only is she losing her daughter, she will lose her apartment and her credit. Only menial jobs will be open to her.

When the scan-chamber opens from outside, brown-shirts sedate the woman and haul her away. Aware that cams are watching him, Harold copies the feed for the evening news so everyone can see. Sanctity of life forbids abortion. Penalties are steep. At least the daughter won't suffer for her mother's crime. Harold isn't convinced.

The next feed shows an Outcast Gray, his scruffy blond beard and tattered gray trench coat hallmarks of non-citizens, who are denied society's benefits. The Board prohibits prostitutes, druggies, murderers, rapists, and other dregs from the Metropolitan domain. Yet here he is in the Loop. Harold shivers. A troop of brown-shirts surrounds the outcast. An Underclass Red woman tries to help him down an alley. She risks a downgrade to Outcast Gray. *Is this love?* Harold wonders.

Brown-shirts shoot the man in the head. The woman goes to her friend, but he is dead. His implant registers no heart or brain activity. As required by law, the patrol has neutralized the terror threat. Each color can downgrade except Outcast Gray. For them, the next step is an overcrowded prison or death. Brown-shirts did him a favor. The Board downgrades the woman to Outcast Gray.

Harold tags another story for evening news feeds, further justification for the new security rules.

All day Harold scans for news, keeping one view on honey-haired Cora and another on the woman who watched her boyfriend die. She should have known that mixed relationships are illegal. He pulls up her file. Several months ago, with Harold's help, the Board downgraded her to Red for associating with an underclass. She welcomed that change until the Board reclassified the man she was with to Outcast Gray. It is easy to move down, almost impossible to move up, unless you are beautiful like honey-haired Cora.

Justice is swift. Brown-shirts take the newly Outcast Gray woman by jet-chopper beyond Metro. From a height of ten feet, they push her out. She lands in swampy wetlands. She struggles to her feet, curses and makes odd hand gestures. Harold's screen doesn't translate, but he remembers his parents using them before they vanished.

Curious, Harold finds a picture of the woman's earlier boyfriend and compares it to the dead man. He finds the similarities as shocking as the differences. It is eerie how downgrading can change a man. The broken nose and sad eyes match, despite the haggard weathered look of what seems like a much older man. Harold adds her earlier transgression to the news as further validation for her adjustment. Harold congratulates himself on his knack for story. Yet he can't help wondering what possessed this woman twice to risk everything. *Is this romantic love?* He shudders at what sacrifices she made.

The next feed is trickier. A Patriot Blue man comes into money, too much says Art-Intel. Lists of transactions pour over Harold's screen, no large sums, but they look suspicious. He doesn't find anything unusual until he thinks of his own spending. Where is the food bill? There are no food charges for months. *Neat trick.*

Scanning back Harold finds where the man previously shopped and looks for unusual activity. He is proud of his ability to track credits forward and back like solving math puzzles. When he hits a dead-end, Harold finds the man on cam and lifts the ID embedded in his silk shirt, something Blues can't afford. Sure enough, a Green woman purchased it with credit from Senator Maverick Lacey. *Got you,* Harold thinks, though it is risky going after an Honorable Purple.

"Harold, my man." A heavy hand presses his shoulder.

A burly African-American, Mel Gardner is Privileged Green, Harold's boss, and director of the Chicago facility. Once a month Mel invites Harold to dinner; picks him up in his vintage Majestic, a Green-approved model. Over steak, Harold endures Mel's complaints about trying to scrape by on a Privileged Green income. Harold can only dream.

Mel practically lifts Harold from his seat, removes Harold's earpiece, and clasps his hand. "You've been selected employee of the month. What do you say?"

Harold is speechless. This is his first. Will it mean a bonus? He has heard of such, though never for a Patriot Blue.

Releasing the handshake, Mel marches off without inviting Harold back to his office. The interruption is brief, leaving Harold feeling special and confused.

When he sits down, the Lacey file is gone. His eyes moisten; he is employee of the month. Has he outperformed coworkers? He wants to compare notes, to talk to someone other than Mel, but his boss forbids him from discussing his work even with coworkers. *You can't tell who might be a traitor,* Mel once said as Harold signed a thick confidentiality agreement in legalese he couldn't begin to understand. He has no one to share his good fortune with.

I am all alone.

Harold pulls up feeds from his apartment and fills all nine views. His home is a Patriot Blue cube like that of his coworkers. He watches their places now and then and is certain they watch his. Rooms are identical down to pale blue décor. If he mistakenly walked into the wrong apartment, he would feel right at home.

His Patriot Blue appliances include micro-cooker, wash/dry unit, and fridge. He has a wall vid with LINC, but only Blue-approved channels: three cooking, two gardening, and eight spiritual that all sound alike. He can watch sitcoms ending with infraction adjustments, news vids, and self-improvement feeds intended to mold him into a model citizen. He has no interest, but they are friends to keep him company at night.

The Privileged Green condos he has seen have a second bedroom, although he can't imagine how he would use it. Appliances are bigger, newer, and more diverse. Green vid LINC accesses more shows. Sometimes he monitors them from work to see what he is missing. Greens can watch wealth-building programs, but nothing that show Harold how he could move up from Patriot Blue.

At least he is not Red. They get efficiency lofts, barely big enough for a bed, cooker, and stacked laundry. Yet even that is better than living on the streets, or being an Outcast Gray. Maybe that woman's dismal prospects are what drove her to help her boyfriend.

Harold pulls up Cora's sitcom and grins. She looks pretty in her lively green floral dress. Before his boss catches him, he changes feeds to the streets and rail station. The monorail loads the last of an early shift of Blues so they can return to their empty apartments. Like him, they micro-cook prepackaged meals, and consume their daily quota of drinks. Then, they sit before the vid for conditioning before another day of work. Harold's shift ends. He doesn't want to be late.

* * *

Grabbing his coat, Harold rushes down three flights of stairs to avoid having to wait for the crowded elevators. In the lobby, he falls in line behind coworkers dressed in a dozen shades of blue to mark their class as they emerge from work. *You don't want anyone mistaking you for Privileged Green, like that could happen.* He doesn't need his coat since he can travel indoors from the office to the monorail and on to his apartment, but someone attacked the monorail last year. To get home, he had to walk five blocks in the cold.

He hurries down the corridor toward the monorail ramps, keeping a watchful eye on brown-shirt guards. *Never draw attention if you don't have to.* When he reaches the turnstile, he sees ahead of him that bun of honey-hair and the sleek shape of Cora's green floral dress. A moment sooner and he might have gathered a whiff of her sweet perfume and risked a hello. She turns with a dreamy smile and boards the Green compartment where he won't be welcome.

Do you recognize me?

He can't share this feeling of belonging with her because he has no hope of that ever happening. He wants no trouble, only to glimpse her and see her safely home. *That is enough,* he tells himself. *Remember, thoughts only remain private when kept to myself.* Yet, memory fades. *If I don't record or share my thoughts, how can I trust they won't disappear?* You can't speak or write without the Standards Board recording everything, so how can you have private thoughts?

His father warned him about the end of privacy, but it didn't seem important at the time. Now that Harold's private thoughts are about Cora, he desperately wants to yell them from the roof terrace, or at least write them on a notepad he hid when the government banned paper. They want to discourage secret messages. Of course, writing anything off the LINC brings adjustments. Mostly, Harold wants to share his thoughts with Cora because of the connection he feels, even though they have only exchanged polite glances.

For two months, since she started acting on her sitcom, Harold has watched the azure-eyed honey-blonde at work and at the monorail. He feels like Romeo wooing Juliet, for she is Privileged Green and he is lowly Blue. He not only doesn't have a chance, any interaction is strictly "verboten." Yet, she has been more pleasant to him than any of his fellow Blues. Like him, they keep their heads down and struggle to get by. He can't stop thinking about her. That is his one private thought, something the state doesn't yet own.

* * *

Harold reaches his desk early the next morning to research Cora. The Standards Board has slated her to become wife to an Honorable Purple, one of several wives, no doubt, since she is Green and the Board permits Purples to have multiple wives like the Biblical patriarchs. She deserves better.

Keeping one of his views on Cora, Harold feels connected, as he hasn't since losing his parents. Back before the Standards Board, he could have approached her and imagined a better life. He longs for those golden days, and imagines his parents would approve of Cora as a daughter-in-law. After all, she is a model, not the naked outcast type, but a model citizen, an exemplar.

Cora's file shows her Patriot Blue parents left her with a Privileged Green family so she could move up. Yet, she is lonely, like Harold. He pulls up history feeds of Cora in her apartment. She cries at her bathroom mirror with water gushing. She must think that drowns out her words: "Mom, Dad, I miss you so much. Why can't I see you?" Why? Because Blues and Greens can't mingle, except under Board-approved conditions like work or at the monorail.

It is at the mirror with water running that Cora shares private thoughts, fears and expectations. She suspects an arranged marriage, which she doesn't want. She longs for someone and as Privileged Green, she is permitted to choose from among other Greens. Yet she keeps to herself. Harold sheds a tear like when his parents left. He hungers for family, but as Patriot Blue, Harold has to wait until the Board chooses for him.

For LINC's sake, they have it wrong. Cora is meant for me. Are you waiting for me to act? If I don't, will I lose you forever?

Daring not to enlarge her image, Harold contents himself with a six-inch screen of her in her dressing room, tablet-writing sitcom notes and rehearsing for her performance. Through the vid-feed, her life unfolds like a movie. She seems so close he could touch her. This is dangerous, but he can't help himself.

Envying the men she performs with, Harold denies her access to leave her dressing room for a moment so he can imprint her image. She looks annoyed, but not angry. Though LINC delays are common, he apologizes in his private thoughts. It is like having to wait longer for the elevator or monorail, one of life's little nuisances. Yet he is touching her, even if only in a manipulative way. He digs his fingernail into his palm. *This is wrong. I have to stop.*

He scans through live city views, sees nothing of interest, and flips back to review her file. Cora struggles more than most Greens. As an entertainer, she hungers for clothes and adornments she can't afford. Harold knows the desire for what you can't have, the burning passion that can be used against you if, LINC forbid, they find you out.

When he returns to Cora's active feed, she isn't in her dressing room or on the set. He locates her leaving by the back door. She looks distraught. He pulls a second feed from across the street and zooms in on her face. Her eyes fill with tears. A history feed shows that moments earlier she received a message that her mother died. She can't attend the funeral since she can't mingle with Blues. A fourth view shows her father at the funeral alone. *Bastards.*

Back on the street, Harold watches three Underclass Reds with scruffy beards. They approach Cora. It isn't safe; she is distracted, not paying attention. Harold sets off an alarm at a nearby jewelry store. That startles the Reds and alerts her. He opens a door for her to a Purple clothier. The Standards Board forbids Greens from this store, but seeing the men, she enters the scan-chamber. She is shaking, terrified. One of the men tries the door. Harold seals it. Brown-shirts pull up in a truck. One Red stumbles and falls against the wall. Blood splatters the back of his shirt. His companions flee. Brown-shirts carry the injured man to the truck.

Harold has no doubt where they will dump him.

Cora looks up toward the camera, forces a smile, and mouths: *thank-you.* She is talking to him. He saved her and she understands. When he releases the door to the street, she leaves, holding her head up as if nothing happened.

"Loitering again?" Mel hangs overhead like a dark cloud.

Harold scrambles the feeds, and lets Art-Intel select his nine views.

Mel blocks the screen. "Dreaming is for fools."

"I wasn't."

Harold scoots back to see his boss' face, but Mel retreats to his office. Harold follows. He tries to figure out how he can challenge what LINC records. He is spending too much time on Cora. He expects another lecture about terror threats and the need for him to focus.

Mel closes the door to his greenly accented office. "You've done your nation a great service." He sits Harold down and stands over him. "But you grow too attached. Wanting what you can't have brings misery. Accept your lot. Let it bring you happiness."

Harold nods. *I should.*

"She does appeal to the eye, doesn't she? I was thinking of approaching her." Mel stares down at Harold, looking for betrayal of private thoughts.

Harold buries his thoughts deeper, but his stomach knots at the thought of his boss approaching Cora when he can't.

"Good. I like you, Harold. You could have a very long

career here. We do vital work. Can you imagine if colors mixed? No, you were too young. We had social strife and terror. No one was safe. It's best that people accept their lot and remove temptations."

Harold plasters a smile on his face as Mel continues, "Remember, Harold, there are no victimless crimes."

What about that Underclass Red woman giving up everything to be with her man, Harold wanted to ask. She wasn't hurting anyone.

"You hear me, Harold? That's why we no longer have lawyers. They create conflict and unhappiness. You don't remember, but I do."

Maybe the cute redhead's mom didn't have an abortion. Maybe someone, like Harold, got bored and wrote her up. Did that Privileged Green couple pay to alter her records so they could take her child? What if rules are arbitrary? What if there are victimless crimes?

Harold begins shaking and falls from his chair.

"Are you okay?" Mel asks, looking concerned.

"I see the light. I know the true path."

Mel helps Harold up. "See, all you needed was an attitude adjustment."

* * *

Ever since he first spotted Cora's honey-hair at the monorail station and received a faint smile in response, Harold conjured ways to approach her. What should he say? How would she react? It would be tricky. Despite listening to her before her mirror, he can't be sure he has all her private thoughts. Then there are ever-present cams. He calls up monorail feeds looking for gaps.

After work, while he waits for the turnstile to accept his implant's signal, Harold fears ending up like that woman who lost her daughter. Then he sees that glow of honey-hair ahead of him. He tries to recall where he found the cams. His brain scrambles with anticipation. He closes his eyes; slows his breathing. Elevated heart rate can cause turnstiles to reject. When the light flashes green, he surges forward.

Harold remembers the cam locations he scanned this morning, but he can't be sure he has found them all. At work, when he found gaps, Art-Intel brought new feeds that weren't there before. As he hurries up the platform, he hears the whir of the monorail. He keeps Cora in the fuzzy edges of his vision so the cams won't pick up that he's following her.

Long sleek cylinders glide into the station, the first Green, several Blue, and aft a small Red compartment. Despite a heated platform, Harold draws his dark overcoat around his collar so that only the bottoms of his trousers show blue. He heads for the first Blue car, which is already filling up. That is the way of life. Blues have crowded compartments, Greens ample space, and Reds pack in like toothpicks, pushing and shoving as befits their class.

Cora lets a pregnant woman and her male companion get into the Green car before her. Harold reaches the first Blue car. Commuters jostle for limited seats. He is ten feet from Cora. She turns, smiles, and disappears inside the Green compartment.

Harold follows her. He recalls a cam gap inside the monorail doors, where he can have a private moment with Cora. He lunges at the opening, stumbles on the step, and falls face first into the aisle at her feet. He gazes up at her green floral dress.

Looking alarmed, she gets to her feet and helps him up. Her touch is firm, but friendly. Her face remains contorted. That is when Harold notices alarms pounding his ears. He forgot the door sensors would reject his implant. He violated the sanctity of Green space. He kisses her hand, a gesture he recalls his father doing with his mom.

Cora pushes him off the train and returns to her seat. Her face carries a dozen messages but mostly fear. Greens scramble off the platform. Shouting, Blues hurry away, abandoning the nearby monorail door. He is a terrorist, having struck terror into the lives of law-abiding citizens. *What have I done?*

A husky brown-shirt runs toward him. Knowing his adjustment will tear him farther from his beloved Cora, Harold runs toward the turnstiles. The Board will downgrade him for sure to Underclass Red; strip him of his job, his apartment, his meager pay. They will make him a desk clerk at the reeducation center, or put him in for reeducation. He would take anything but interrogation where they would dig at his private thoughts.

Angry voices pelt him from behind. How can he be so rude, so Blue? Knowing turnstiles will reject him, Harold leaps over, ripping his overcoat on the metal bridge. Pushing through the bewildered crowd trying to get to the platform, he races downstairs. He breaks out onto the nearly empty boulevard. Red dregs scurry about, cleaning the streets. Harold runs as hard as he can. Cold wind slaps his face. He feels alive. His heart thumps in his chest. He can only imagine the medical stream his implant is providing. He remembers the Outcast Gray man trying to escape and getting shot. *Bad plan.*

Sirens approach. There is no escape. Harold is on every surveillance feed. Dozens like him back at the office will follow his movements, check his history, and measure his heart rate and brain waves. *Why did I do this? One smile from that angelic face and I ruined my life. What about Cora? Will they adjust you for my recklessness? What will you tell them when they interrogate you?*

He wants to reach her to tell her how sorry he is. He aches to keep them from hurting her. But they will track him through his implant, wherever he goes. Instinct sets in, self-preservation. Seeing brown-shirts, Harold darts into an alley where Reds cluster. Theirs is a desperate place for marginal lives. He has seen morality vids of Blues straying into Red neighborhoods. Harold is ready to collapse from fright, but isn't he about to join them?

Voices yell from behind. "Stop before your adjustment gets worse."

Harold runs. He believes he can get away, yet knows that he can't. How can he hold two divergent beliefs at the same time? This new sensation spurs him on. He is desperate, terrified, a terrorist. Yet what presses into his mind is Cora wanting a better life.

He trips or falls; maybe someone shoved him. He can't be sure. Instead of hitting the ground, he flies through a doorway. Moments blur with strange images—filth he has never seen except on vid. His nostrils pinch, trying to choke off the putrid stench of rotten food and garbage. Smoke burns his eyes. His skin feels as if covered in stinging ants. How can people live like this? He loses his footing; keeps moving, half running, half carried. Stairs lead down and down as if entering the underworld.

When he comes to a stop, bright lights blind him. A faceless, mud-haired woman breaks into view. Harold recalls the woman who tried to protect her companion. He is convinced it is the same couple he helped catch last year.

"Who are you? What do you want?"

* * *

Despite having seen adjustments on vid-feed, it still astounds Harold how quickly his status can change. One moment you are minding your own business, in a life you have adapted to. Then it is gone. You have no job, no credits. You lose your home. You can't show your face. You are a lost soul at the mercy of powers you cannot control. Beat down, you will do as they ask for to resist is pointless.

While Brown-shirts escort Harold to interrogation, he plays over in his mind all the lives he has watched change. He can't stop thinking of Cora. He has to see her.

Brown-shirts march him down a bland beige corridor he has never seen before. Lights become dimmer until he has to strain to see the stain-marked floor. They thrust him into a room bathed in light so bright he closes his eyes tight and sees black brightness.

After the door slams, Harold hears a familiar bass voice. "I warned you obsession would lead to despair."

Sweating, Harold stands on shaky legs. His eyes cannot adjust in a room bathed in white, as if every inch of wall, floor and ceiling radiates heat. He has no perspective as to whether the room is large or small. He cannot see Mel; can't tell if there is a table or chair. Harold shakes too much to bring himself to ask.

"I had high hopes for you, Harold. You do good work, but this obsession shames you. You see that, don't you?"

Harold nods. He likes easy questions that he can answer. He is glad he can't see his boss, yet feels that presence hover nearby, over his shoulder.

"Speak up! Say the words."

"I … see." Harold squints, because he can't see. His knees want to buckle, but he dare not ask for a seat.

"You've not only shamed yourself, you've embarrassed me. You forced the Board to act on behalf of the woman. Observe the extent and repercussions of your crime."

Lights dim. The wall morphs into a room with a table and two chairs. Cora sits across from a gray-haired man, a Privileged Green by his clothes. Harold approaches. As he crosses his chamber, the image shimmers and fades. His hand reaches for Cora. Realizing his mistake, he slaps it to his side.

The gray-hair says, "You know your crime, don't you?"

"The man tripped."

The gray-hair leans toward her. "He saved your life. Surely, you knew. You even thanked him. You've grown fond of him, haven't you?"

"How could I? We've never met."

Behind the gray-hair, the screen shows her acknowledging Harold's hello. "Come now, Cora. You know what happens if your reputation is tarnished? Have you thought about this man?"

"Absolutely not!" Looking terrified, she brushes honey

hair from her face. The Board can downgrade her for not living up to the Green code of conduct. "He reminded me of my brother. I haven't seen him since—"

"Since you were elevated to Privileged Green." The gray-hair's face softens. "Lucky for you an Honorable Purple wants you as his wife. You'll gain status and can escape the Blues."

Her face turns sour. Harold gave the Board the leverage to force her into a marriage she doesn't want. If she gives herself to this Purple, all will be forgiven. But Green wives aren't accepted into Purple society, particularly those elevated from Blue. She will be isolated and miserable. That will be her adjustment and there is nothing Harold can do.

Cora nods somberly. "Can I meet him first?"

"I'm sure you know him. It's Senator Lacey." The gray-hair holds out his hand to close the deal.

She expected this, Harold knows from her mirror-talk, but there is no joy in her face. Maverick Lacey is married to a Purple. Cora will be no more than his mistress, one of many. Walking toward her image, Harold looks for an exit, as if breaking free he would know where to find her. She is too good for this. That is when he realizes she was elevated from Blue to Green for this very purpose. Anger surfaces, stiffening his quivering jaw. He tries to wash this away before his implant betrays him.

"Come now, Cora," the gray-hair says. "You've contaminated yourself by associating with a Blue. This great outcome is available because we caught things in time."

"I … I'll marry the senator."

"Good." Gray-hair grins his victory.

The image morphs to a small chapel. Time has passed. Cora stands with Senator Maverick Lacey, the womanizer. She looks angelic, innocent, frightened. Harold's knees buckle; he falls to the floor. He expects her to notice and come to his aid, but she isn't really here.

"You shame yourself," Mel's voice echoes. "You betray your deepest thoughts. You cannot hide them from me."

Lying on the floor, Harold watches Senator Lacey kiss the bride. It is a tiny wedding—the couple, gray-hair, and a preacher who looks like an old-style lawyer. Tears stream down Harold's cheeks as he watches Lacey escort his Cora away.

The image vanishes and light bathes the room again. Harold wipes his cheeks.

"You are fortunate," Mel's disembodied voice says. "She's gone as temptation. No more sitcom. You'll lose a month's credits, but I'll let you keep your job if you behave. You came close to losing everything. Don't disappoint me again."

"Bless you, oh privileged one," Harold mutters. "Bless you for your wisdom, benevolence, and for my modest adjustment."

Harold suppressed his private thoughts so deep he fears never retrieving them again, but they rattle around, like an energized ping-pong ball. *Damn the color-classes.* Cora won't be happy as a second or third wife, mistress really. Harold wonders if Mel knows he is thinking of setting her free, no matter what the risk.

The End

OTHER STORIES BY LANCE ERLICK

THE REBEL WITHIN (novel)

After the Second American Civil War, the Federal Union pursues a world without men by rounding up the remaining males.

Annabelle is a tomboy who lost her parents at age three. Despite her rebellious acts against a conformist society, the state pushes her to become a cop intern at age 16 to catch escaped boys. Then she's forced to choose between joining the elite military unit that took her parents or being torn from her beloved sister and adoptive mom. Meanwhile, she meets a handsome boy who escaped prison, and helps him get away.

While facing a cop intern boss who hates her, a military commander who demands too much, and an amazon bully who won't leave her alone, Annabelle struggles with conscience. Will she risk everything by hunting for her imprisoned birth mother and helping escaped boys avoid the federal roundup? Can she stand up to the amazon? Will she survive the rigorous military qualifying program so she won't be sent away, while remaining true to herself and protecting her family?

Will she cross paths with that handsome boy again?

REBELS DIVIDED (novel) – Three Years Later

After the Second American Civil War, a nation divided. The Federal Union controls most of the country enforcing harmony and an all-female society with the help of EggFusion Fertilization and Female Mechanized Warriors based near Knoxville. The male-dominated Appalachian Outland promotes rugged individualism, but Thane Edwards has a monopoly of power, church, and the economy. He enforces this with his Rangers, loosely modeled on the legendary Texas Rangers. The governor of

Tenn-tucky and the Outland warlord conclude a secret deal that each believes will enhance their power.

Geo is a Daniel Boone type frontiersman who hungers to see more of the world than the tiny impoverished Outland glen where he and his pa hide from local Rangers. Geo fights Union mechs and Outland Rangers to protect friends, neighbors, and refugees fleeing the Federal Union and Ranger brutality.

Annabelle is a tough yet fragile tomboy who lost her parents at age three and was raised by Geo's estranged Mom. Annabelle develops a rebellious streak in her conformist society (Federal Union). She becomes a mech warrior to see the forbidden Outland. When she refuses a politically arranged marriage to the Outland warlord, he kidnaps her and her adopted sister.

Pursued by Union mechs and Outland Rangers, Geo and Annabelle must come together to rescue her sister and gain justice for his pa's murder. While trying to survive, can they trust growing feelings for each other despite being sworn enemies?

ABOUT THE AUTHOR

Raised by a roaming aerospace engineer, Lance Erlick grew up in various parts of the United States and Europe. He took to stories as his anchor and was inspired by his father's engineering work on cutting-edge aerospace projects to look to the future. He writes speculative fiction, science fiction, dystopian and young adult and likes to explore the future implications of social and technological trends.

Find out more about the author and his work at LanceErlick.com.

www.ingramcontent.com/pod-product-compliance
Lightning Source LLC
Chambersburg PA
CBHW071630140626
46555CB00021B/1944